Stephanie Blake

Poo
Bum

GECKO PRESS

Once
there was
a little rabbit
who could
only say
one
thing...

Poo
bum

Every morning
when his mother said,
"Time to get up,
my little rabbit,"
he would reply:

Poo
bum

At lunchtime
when his father said,
"Eat your spinach,
my little rabbit,"
he would reply:

Poo
bum

At night
when his big sister said,
"Come and have your
bath, my little rabbit,"
he would reply:

Poo
bum

One day
a wolf asked him,
"May I eat you,
my little rabbit?"
And he replied:

Poo
bum

And so
the wolf
ate
the little rabbit.

When the wolf
went home,
his wife asked,
"How are you,
my dear?"
The wolf replied:

Poo
bum

That night,
the wolf wasn't
feeling well.
He called
the doctor.

The doctor said,
"Say ah!"

The wolf replied,
"Poo bum!"

The doctor cried,
"What!
You've eaten
my little rabbit!"

The
very brave
doctor
went looking
for his
little rabbit.

He pulled the little rabbit out
and said, "Oh!
My little poo bum!"

The little rabbit
was shocked.
He exclaimed,
"Good heavens, Father!
How dare you call me that?
You know perfectly well
my name is
Simon."

Back at home
his mother said,
"Eat your soup,
my little rabbit."
He replied,
"Of course, Mother!
The flavour is exquisite!"

The next morning,
when his father said,
"Brush your teeth,
my little rabbit,"
he replied:

Fart!

This edition first published in 2011 by Gecko Press
PO Box 9335, Marion Square, Wellington 6141, New Zealand
info@geckopress.com

Reprinted 2012 (twice), 2013 (twice), 2014 (twice)

English language edition © Gecko Press Ltd 2011

All rights reserved. No part of this publication may be reproduced or transmitted
or utilised in any form, or by any means, electronic, mechanical, photocopying or otherwise
without the prior written permission of the publisher.

Original title: Caca boudin
Text and illustrations by Stephanie Blake
© 2002, l'ecole des loisirs, Paris

A catalogue record for this book is available from the National Library of New Zealand.

Translated by Linda Burgess
Edited by Penelope Todd
Typesetting by Luke Kelly, New Zealand
Printed by Everbest, China

ISBN hardback: 978-1-877467-96-7
ISBN paperback: 978-1-877467-97-4

For more curiously good books, visit www.geckopress.com